SNOWBALL

Nina Crews

Greenwillow Books, New York

The art was prepared as collages made from full-color photographs. The text type is Franklin Gothic ITC Medium.   Copyright © 1997 by Nina Crews.
All rights reserved. Published by Greenwillow Books, a division of William Morrow & Company, Inc., 1350 Avenue of the Americas, New York, NY 10019.
Printed in Hong Kong by South China Printing Company (1988) Ltd.   First Edition   10 9 8 7 6 5 4 3 2 1
Library of Congress Cataloging-in-Publication Data.   Crews, Nina.   Snowball / by Nina Crews.   p.   cm.   ISBN 0-688-14928-6 (trade).
ISBN 0-688-14929-4 (lib. bdg.)   [1. Snow—Fiction.]   I. Title.   PZ7.C8683Nj 1997   [E]—dc21   96-48180   CIP   AC

FOR ANN AND DONALD | Special thanks to Hannah Hodson, who is featured in this book, and her parents, Kerris and Ed Hodson; to Justine McGovern, for all her child wrangling and contacts; to Jesstine Porter and Curtis Griffith of the Prospect Park Pre-School; and to all the children who played in the snow with us: Emily Corwin, Nathaniel Elkins, Daniella Grant, Ivy Johnson, Frank Ling, Daniel Penny, Andy Reich, De'Andra Rivers, Nailah Stackhouse, Hannah Wurgart, and Jesse Zalewski.

It's Monday morning. The weather report says "Snow."

But the sky is clear and blue all day.

Sand & Water

It doesn't snow on Tuesday either,

and Wednesday's cold and gray.

Thursday night I dream a perfect snowball.

Friday morning I want to stay in bed.

Instead, I look outside.

Snow! It's everywhere.

It falls up, down, and sideways all morning.

When it stops, I collect it.

I make a perfect snowball.

I throw it high. Maybe it will fly . . .

but it comes crashing down!

I think this one will be dinner. Perfect.